Make Way for the Queen!

A humorous story

This edition first published in 2006 by
Sea-to-Sea Publications
1980 Lookout Drive
North Mankato
Minnesota 56003

Printed in China

Library of Congress Cataloging-in-Publication Data:

Harvey, Damian.
  Make way for the queen! / by Damian Harvey.
    p. cm. — (Reading corner)
  Summary: Upon hearing that the queen is coming, each animal and all the townspeople
envision very different looking royal visitors.
  ISBN 1-59771-012-1
    [1. Kings, queens, rulers, etc.—Fiction. 2. Animals—Fiction.] I. Title. II. Series.

PZ7.H267473Mak 2005
[E]—dc22

                                                                    2004063195

9 8 7 6 5 4 3 2

Published by arrangement with the Watts Publishing Group Ltd, London

Series Editor: Jackie Hamley
Series Advisors: Linda Gambrell, Dr. Barrie Wade, Dr. Hilary Minns
Design: Peter Scoulding

Make Way for the Queen!

Written by
Damian Harvey

Illustrated by
Jo Brown

SEA-TO-SEA
Mankato Collingwood London

Damian Harvey

"I enjoy writing stories that have a surprise in them. Lots of people get a surprise in this story!"

Jo Brown

"I really enjoyed illustrating this book. I love to draw animals, especially cats. I have three-two are kittens."

Ant looked over a hill and saw the Queen coming.

Ant ran to tell Mouse.
"Make way for the
Queen!" chirped Ant.

6

Mouse ran to tell Cat.
"Make way for the Queen!"
squeaked Mouse.

Cat ran to tell Dog.
"Make way for the
Queen!" meowed Cat.

Dog ran to tell Horse.
"Make way for the
Queen!" barked Dog.

12

Horse ran to tell the
farmer. "Make way for the
Queen!" neighed Horse.

15

The farmer told the whole town. "Here comes the Queen!" shouted the farmer.

Everyone came
to cheer the
Queen.

The Queen and her ants
walked slowly into town.

And Ant waved
and cheered!

22

Notes for parents and teachers

READING CORNER has been structured to provide maximum support for new readers. The stories may be used by adults for sharing with young children. Primarily, however, the stories are designed for newly independent readers, whether they are reading these books in bed at night, or in the reading corner at school or in the library.

Starting to read alone can be a daunting prospect. READING CORNER helps by providing visual support and repeating words and phrases, while making reading enjoyable. These books will develop confidence in the new reader, and encourage a love of reading that will last a lifetime!

If you are reading this book with a child, here are a few tips:

1. Make reading fun! Choose a time to read when you and the child are relaxed and have time to share the story.

2. Encourage children to reread the story, and to retell the story in their own words, using the illustrations to remind them what has happened.

3. Give praise! Remember that small mistakes need not always be corrected.

READING CORNER covers three grades of early reading ability, with three levels at each grade. Each level has a certain number of words per story, indicated by the number of bars on the spine of the book, to allow you to choose the right book for a young reader:

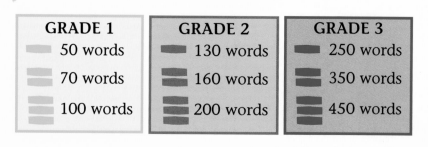

GRADE 1	GRADE 2	GRADE 3
50 words	130 words	250 words
70 words	160 words	350 words
100 words	200 words	450 words